The Gingerbread Man

Parragon

Bath • New York • Cologne • Melbourne • Delhi
Hong Kong • Shenzhen • Singapore • Amsterdam

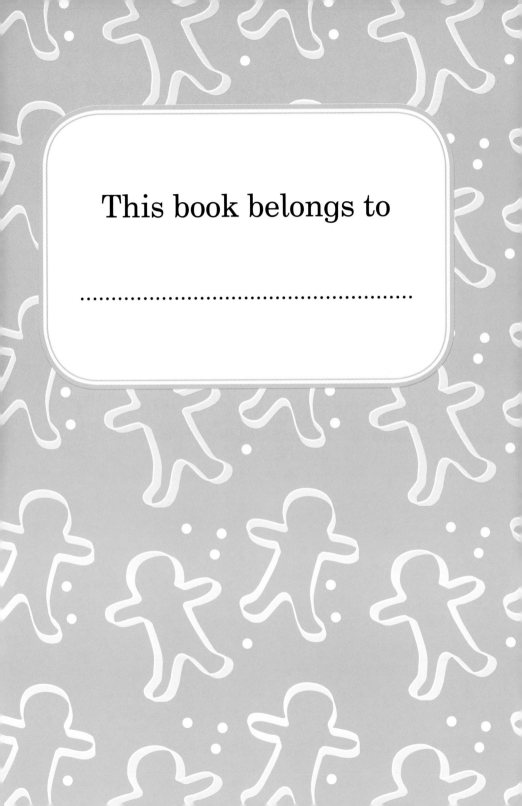

This book belongs to

....

This edition published by Parragon Books Ltd in 2015 and distributed by

Parragon Inc.
440 Park Avenue South, 13th Floor
New York, NY 10016
www.parragon.com

Illustrated by Gail Yerrill
Reading consultant: Geraldine Taylor

ISBN 978-1-4748-0821-7

Printed in China

The Gingerbread Man

Five steps for enjoyable reading

Traditional stories and fairy tales are a great way to begin reading practice. The stories and characters are familiar and lively. Follow the steps below to help your child become a confident and independent reader:

One sunny day, the little old woman looked in her cookbook. "I'll bake a gingerbread man," she decided. So she mixed and rolled and cut out the gingerbread man. Then she popped him in the ove

8

Step 1
Read the story aloud to your child. Run your finger under the words as you read.

Step 2
Look at the pictures and talk about what is happening.

Step 3
Read the simple text on the right-hand page together. When reading, some words come up again and again, such as **the**, **to**, **and**. Your child will quickly get to recognize these high-frequency words by sight.

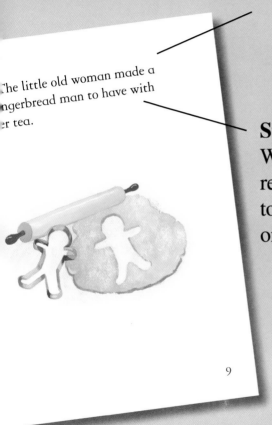

The little old woman made a gingerbread man to have with her tea.

9

Step 4
When your child is ready, encourage them to read the simple lines on their own.

Step 5
Help your child to complete the puzzles at the back of the book.

One sunny day, the little old woman looked in her cookbook.

"I'll bake a gingerbread man," she decided. So she mixed and rolled and cut out the gingerbread man. Then she popped him in the oven.

The little old woman made a
gingerbread man to have with
her tea.

But, oh dear! When the little old woman opened the oven door, she had a big surprise. The gingerbread man jumped up and ran out through the door.

"Come back!" she called.

"You are not going to eat me!" said the gingerbread man.

The gingerbread man ran
away down the road.

The little old
woman and the little
old man chased after
the gingerbread man.

"Run, run, as fast as
you can. You can't catch
me, I'm the gingerbread
man!" he laughed.

"A pig can't eat me," he said.

The little old woman,
the little old man, and
the pig chased after the
gingerbread man.

"A cow can't eat me," he said.

"Run, run, as fast as you can.
You can't catch me, I'm the
gingerbread man!" he laughed.

The little old woman, the little
old man, the pig, and the cow
all chased after the
gingerbread man.

He ran past
the horse.

"You are big, but I am fast," he said.

"Run, run, as fast as you can. You can't catch me, I'm the gingerbread man!" he laughed. The little old woman, the little old man, the pig, the cow, and the horse all chased after the gingerbread man.

The gingerbread man ran as fast as he could.

Soon, the gingerbread man
came to a river.
"Oh no, how will I get
across?" he cried.

"I will help you," said the fox.

"Hold on to my tail," said the fox. So the gingerbread man held on to the fox's tail. The fox jumped into the water.

"I will get wet," cried the
gingerbread man.

"Jump onto my back," said the fox. So the gingerbread man jumped onto the fox's back.

The gingerbread man saw the little old woman, the little old man, the pig, the cow, and the horse far behind him.

"Now they can't eat me," he said.

"You are getting heavy," said the fox. "Jump onto my nose." So the gingerbread man jumped onto the fox's nose.

But it was a trick! As soon as they were safely on the other side of the river, the fox tossed the gingerbread man into the air ... and gobbled him up!

And that was the end of the gingerbread man.

Puzzle time!

Which two words rhyme?

man big fox run pig

Which word does not match
the picture?

tail

nose

oven

Which word matches the picture?

how

cow

now

Who bakes the gingerbread man?

little old woman

little old man

horse

Which sentence is right?

You can't catch me.

You can catch me.